D1360226

CUENTO
DE LUZ

To Marc, Yuna, Adriel, and Laia: so that they can have the most incredible adventures together.
- Susanna Isern -

To my parents.
- Marta Chicote -

Waterproof and tear resistant.
Produced without water, without trees and without bleach.
Saves 50% of energy compared to normal paper.

The Music of the Sea
Text © 2017 Susanna Isern
Illustrations © 2017 Marta Chicote
This edition © 2017 Cuento de Luz SL
Calle Claveles, 10 | Urb. Monteclaro | Pozuelo de Alarcón | 28223 | Madrid | Spain
www.cuentodeluz.com
Title in Spanish: La música del mar
English translation by Jon Brokenbow
Printed in PRC by Shanghai Chenxi Printing Co., Ltd. February 2017, print number 1663-5
ISBN: 978-84-16733-28-6
All rights reserved

3 1489 00701 9472

The Music
of the Sea

Susanna Isern   **Marta Chicote**

FREEPORT MEMORIAL LIBRARY

Lemonsea was a little seaside village. It had an old chapel, without a bell, and four tiny cabins.

Though it was only a little village, it was full of life. The villagers spent their days in the streets, and the children played happily on the seashore.

One day, Lemonsea was hit by a huge storm. Rain flooded the land, and a wild wind destroyed all of the crops. It blew away all the villagers' boats, and tore the roofs off the houses. But worst of all, it frightened away the fish, who swam off to find calmer waters.

From that day on, there was nothing left to catch along that whole stretch of coastline. Little by little, the families left the village to find a new home.

In a small, blue cabin lived Daniel and his daughter, Marina. He was a very stubborn fisherman, and he had decided to stay put. He was sure that sooner or later, the fish would return.

But Marina didn't understand why her father wanted to stay in the nearly deserted village. She felt sad and lonely, as all of her friends had left.

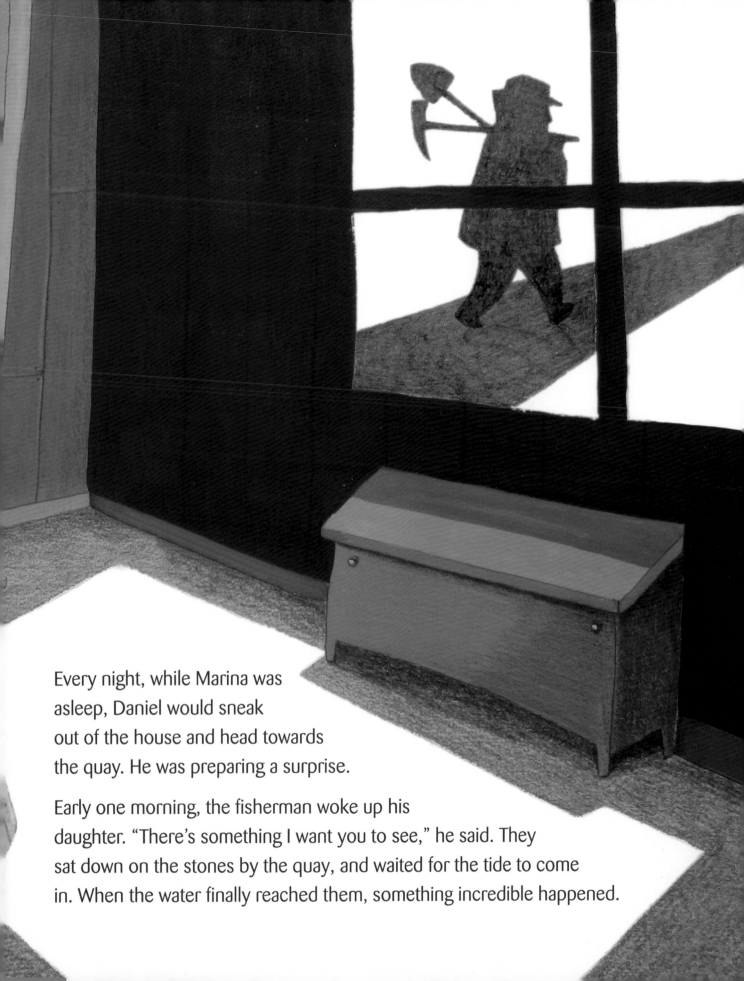

Every night, while Marina was
asleep, Daniel would sneak
out of the house and head towards
the quay. He was preparing a surprise.

Early one morning, the fisherman woke up his
daughter. "There's something I want you to see," he said. They
sat down on the stones by the quay, and waited for the tide to come
in. When the water finally reached them, something incredible happened.

Strange, beautiful music began to play. It washed over the waves, flowed between the houses, rose into the sky, and drifted far, far away. It was a deep, captivating sound, mysterious and unique. "My gift to you is the music of the sea," said the fisherman, with tears in his eyes.

Daniel had cleverly drilled pipes into the quay, creating a wonderful sea organ. The sea played this instrument with its waves, its currents, and its tides, accompanied by the wind.

From that moment on, Marina enjoyed life in Lemonsea much, much more.
The ever-changing music of the sea was there to keep her company.

Sometimes it reminded her of church bells, and other times of a great ship
sailing towards the village. Once she imagined it was a choir of children
singing together, and even a great opera.

One night, she was woken by a new, very different melody. Marina ran down to the quay, so that she could hear it more clearly.

Mysterious voices were accompanying the music. Marina looked out to sea, confused, when all of a sudden she saw something huge and glittering rise up out of the water. Two beautiful white whales were floating on the surface. They were dancing and singing to the sound of the sea organ.

Its music had drawn them to Lemonsea.

From that day on, whenever the sky filled with stars, Marina would get out of bed to watch the wonderful performance. Until one night, one of the whales drew up alongside the quay, as if it were a great ship. That night, and many more besides, Marina sailed far out to sea with the whales. She would lie down, and as she listened to the music of the sea, she would fall fast asleep.

She would bathe in the light of the moon and
the stars until the sun rose over the horizon,
and the whales took her back to the shore.

The arrival of the whales made Marina happy to be in Lemonsea again. But as the days went by, Daniel began to lose hope that the fish would ever return, and finally he decided to leave the village.

One morning, they climbed on board their boat. Marina felt sad, and did not want to go. That day, the sea was playing a strangely beautiful song. It didn't seem to be saying goodbye to them, but quite the opposite.

Daniel began to row, but no matter how hard he tried, they couldn't move forward. With puzzled expressions, the father and daughter looked down into the water. What they saw left them absolutely amazed.

Hundreds of fish had surrounded the boat, preventing it from moving. The sea, its music, and the song of the whales, had brought them back to Lemonsea.

The fish had returned, and they were soon followed by the villagers who had left. Everyone was talking about the abundance of the waters, and the magical music that could be heard there.

And that was how Lemonsea grew into a large town with a school, lots of streets, and a big church with a bell tower.

And every night, Marina would head out to sea
with the whales. She would lie on their backs, and as she listened to the music
of the sea, she would fall fast asleep. She would bathe in the light of the moon
and the stars until the sun rose, and they took her back to the shore.

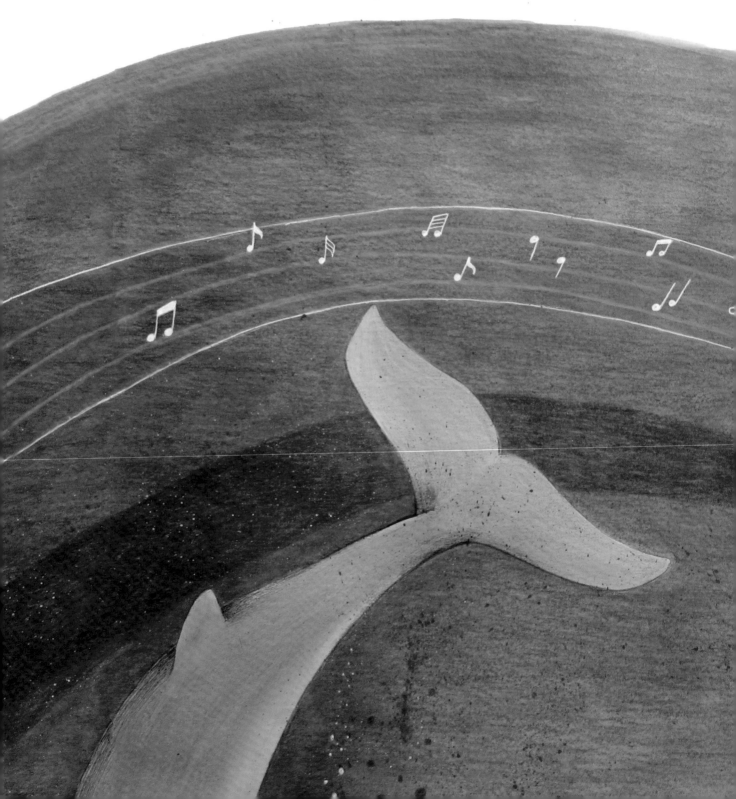

DISCARDED BY
FREEPORT
MEMORIAL LIBRARY

FREEPORT MEMORIAL LIBRARY
CHILDREN'S ROOM